The Pleasure Contract

The Pleasure Contract

A steamy Novella by Vannah Reign

Published by Vannah Reign Books
First Edition – June 2025
ISBN: 979-8-9987240-1-5

For permissions or inquiries, contact:
Email:
vannahreign@thepleasurecontract.com
Website: www.thepleasurecontract.com

Printed in the United States of America

About the author

Vannah Reign is a woman who writes from experience, heart, and imagination—a storyteller who understands that pleasure, power, and passion often live in the same room. A professional woman, a nurturer by nature, and a bold spirit by choice, Vannah brings the perfect mix of confidence, vulnerability, fantasy and raw honesty to her writing.

With a love for words and an eye for life's complicated edges, she explores the spaces where desire meets truth—where love and lust aren't always clean, but they're always real. Her stories speak to the grown woman who's been through some things, the woman who knows what it feels like to give too much, and the one who's finally learning to choose herself first.

Vannah believes in telling it like it is—with a little finesse, a lot of passion, and always a touch of grace. When she's not writing, she's manifesting joy, working hard, loving deeply, and staying true to who she is: a woman who knows her worth and isn't afraid to own it.

The Pleasure Contract is her debut novella—a steamy, unapologetic journey into the gray area between what feels good and what makes sense.

Dedication

For every woman who's ever given too much, wanted more, or loved in silence.

To the one who knew better but stayed anyway.

To the one who swore it was just sex—but caught feelings.

To the one who finally walked away.

Hell, this is even dedicated to the versions of myself I had to outgrow.

This book is for you.

This book is for us.

Acknowledgements

Shoutout to every grown woman who's ever tried to keep it casual and got caught up.

You're not crazy, sis—you're just human. And I see you.

To the stories that wrote me before I ever wrote this book—thank you for the heartbreak, the heat, and the healing.

To the one who pushed me to write it.

To my tribe, my cheerleaders, and even the ones who ghosted me—thank you for showing me who I am (and who I'll never be again).

Love,

Author Reign

Table of contents

Entanglements
don't come with
instructions...

Just consequences.

Chapter One: No Strings, Just Fire

I told myself I wasn't calling him again.

I said I'd block his number, delete the messages, and pretend like his dick hadn't changed the way I breathe.

But here I am-one leg up, the other stretched out, his hands gripping my thighs like I'm something he paid for.

He's saying shit like "*You mine. Say it.*" And I hate how fast my mouth obeys when my pride swore it wouldn't.

This isn't love.

It's something louder.

Something we both didn't sign up for.

I mean—I've got a man. He's got a girl.

Yet here I am, screaming "**fuck that bitch**" while my body trembles, spilling over his monster dick like it belongs to me.

He's got one hand lightly wrapped around my neck, the other gripping my hip like it might disappear.

"*You my lil freak, huh?*" he growls into my ear.

"You a freak for zaddy?"

Each word hits deeper.

So does he.

"*You mine,*" he says through gritted teeth, pounding me harder like he's trying to prove it.

I twist my face toward him, lips parted, eyes wild.

"***Then act like it.***"

He goes still for a second. Just one.

Like the words sank in deeper than his dick ever could.

Then he grabs a fistful of my hair, pulls me back just enough to whisper in my ear, "**Shut the fuck up and take this dick.**"

And I do.

Because what else can I do when every part of me-heart, body, pride-melts under him?

His hips slam against mine like punishment and pleasure at once. The rhythm's wild now, like he's trying to fuck the defiance out of me. And maybe he is.

"*Don't ever ignore me again,*" he says through clenched teeth.

He says it again. And again.

Each stroke timed with his words.

"Don't. Ever. Ignore. Me. Again."

"Don't ever take my pussy away from me."

I want to talk back, but my mouth is too busy moaning his name.

And when I finally whisper it, *"Legend..."*—he stops.

"What, baby?"

That voice. That tone. That softness that only shows up between the filth.

I catch my breath and murmur, *"Fuck this pussy."*

His response? A slow stroke. Then a growl.

"Oh, it's this pussy?"

He starts again, harder.

Meaner.

"*Say it's my pussy.*"

"*It's your pussy baby!*"

He slows, leans down, kisses my mouth so intimately, like I'm something sacred.

"*Yea, you my bitch, ain't you? Ain't you?*"

"You know this pussy mine."

He grabbed my hair tighter, pulled me back, and said:

"*Say it louder.*"

I moaned it this time.

He groaned and fucked me deeper

"*Shut the fuck up and take this monster cock.*"

"*Yeah, keep acting like you don't want it.*"

"*You a freak ass bitch for me.*"

"Yeah. Just for you." I said.

"Say it."

"Just for you, Zaddy."

He growled and stroked even deeper.

That thick-ass dick making me shake.

My eyes rolled back. My legs gave out.

I was gone.

And then he said:

"Now tell me you my hoe."

And I did.

I didn't even hesitate.

"I'm your hoe."

"Yeah, you my bitch."

"My hoe ass bitch"

"These niggas ain't built like me, huh?"

"Tell me."

"No, baby they not."

He started fucking me so hard I couldn't even speak.

Couldn't breathe.

Couldn't think.

And when I came, he came with me.

Right behind me, moaning into my neck:

"Don't ever fucking ignore me again."

"I was trying to come fuck you. You ain't wanna get fucked?"

"What—you had another dick, huh?

Tell me."

I was speechless.

Shaking.

Eyes full of tears from how deep
he'd gone.

And then, while catching his breath,
he whispered:

"*You sexy fuck. I'm a nasty-ass
nigga for you.*"

And you my lil freak.

And I knew I was gone.

This was supposed to be nothing.

Just sex.

But I was deep in already.

And I didn't know how to get out.

And just like that, the war between

us fades... for now.

We lay there in silence.

His breathing heavy against my neck, skin slick with sweat, his hand still gripping my thigh like he's not ready to let me go—not even a little.

I should've said something.

Like, I can't keep doing this. Or, What are we really doing?

But instead, I stare at the ceiling, trying to slow the spin in my chest that has nothing to do with the orgasm and everything to do with him.

He finally speaks.

"Damn…. We goin' back to work Monday?"

I smirk. "Yeah. Eight to four. Every day."

He shifts, kisses the side of my neck like he ain't just rearranged my insides minutes ago.

"Damn,

" He says again. Like he doesn't like the idea of me being anywhere but here.

I turn to face him, a little attitude in my tone. "*You be playin' with me.*"

That does it.

He props himself up on one elbow, that cocky-ass smirk gone.

"*Stop fuckin' saying that.*"

His eyes are locked on mine now. Intense.

Focused.

"*Just say what you want. You want the dick? Say that.*"

I raise an eyebrow. "Say it just like that?"

"Exactly like that."

He leans in, voice low and filthy. "*Say 'come give me that dick,' and I'm there.*"

I laugh, try to play it off. "*You don't really care about me. All you care about is her.*"

His whole face changes.

That switch.

"***You crazy as hell.***"

He grabs my chin gently but firmly. "*You my bitch.*"

His voice is rough, but his eyes... Soft. Searching.

"*Crazy as hell,*" he repeats. Like he can't believe I'd even question it.

I look at him, eyes narrow, heart thumping. *"Then act like it "*

There's a pause. Heavy. Hanging.

For a second, I think I went too far.

But then he smiles-slow, dirty.

"I love when you talk back."

And just like that, he's back on top of me again.

The next morning the sun creeps through the blinds like it's got questions I don't feel like answering.

His arm is still draped over me, heavy and warm, like he forgot this wasn't supposed to mean anything.

I don't move. Not right away.

Because truth is... I don't want to.

He stirs, groans a little, voice still thick with sleep.

"You still here?"

I roll my eyes with a smile. *"You still talkin'?"*

He smirks, eyes still closed. *"You still mine?"*

My chest tightens. Just a little.

But I play it off.

"Don't start."

He turns over, pulling me into him like he owns the right.

"Say it."

His lips are right at my ear now.

"Say I'm your fuckin' nigga."

"Legend"

"Say it."

I Laugh, low and soft. **"You ma nigga"**.

That shit turned him on

He kisses my shoulder, then my neck.

Then slides his hand down, fingers parting me slow, like he ain't already had it twice.

He starts pleasuring me with his tongue...

"Good. 'Cause you already know you my bitch."

I shake my head, biting my lip. **"You got a girl."**

He doesn't stop. Doesn't blink.

"He says, **and I don't give a fuck.**"

This the pussy I want, tongue
kissing me. And then he says it
again

This. The. Pussy. I. Want

The words land harder than they
should. And just like that...

My body betrays me again.

Arching. Opening. Begging.
Squirting...

Chapter Two: When I Really Saw Him

Now, i'd seen him before. A few times, actually.

But that day-*that* day-I saw him differently.

He stood at the front of the room, giving a speech about mentoring young men and helping them find jobs, and I don't know if it was the way his voice carried through the space or the way he filled out that suit, but something hit me in my chest and my thighs at the same damn time. His name was Legend.

Light-skinned. Bald-headed. Caramel complexion so smooth you could taste it just looking at him.

That grown man build-fit like he hits the gym but doesn't live there. Well-spoken. Clean-cut.

Dressed like a man who knows who he is.

Confidence in every step, every pause between his words. He had that *quiet* power that made women straighten up in their seats and try not to stare too long.

And me? Fresh out of a 16-year marriage with a man who barely looked at me like that. So yeah...

I saw him with **single eyes** for the first time. Hungry eyes. Curious eyes. And boy, wasn't he fine.

I started telling the girls at work about my little crush. Just casual. Flirty whispers at lunch.

"Girl, that man is sexy. Smooth as hell."

"I don't know what he's got going on, but he could get it."

What I didn't know was that he'd already been talking about me.

Turns out, he told one of my co-worker's husbands that he thought I was beautiful. Said he wanted me. Said he'd been watching me too-quietly. That part made my stomach flip when I found out. The feeling was mutual. We were circling each other without even knowing it.

But then weeks passed... and I didn't see him again.

He didn't show up to any meetings, no hallway sightings, no run-ins in the break room. I started wondering if he was even still around. I searched his name on Facebook-nothing. Looked for him in the system at work-still nothing. It started to feel silly, but something in me wanted to find him.

Then one of the girls said, "*Why don't you try Instagram? Everybody's on Instagram.*"

I rolled my eyes, but I did it. Typed in his name... and there he was.

Profile clean. Laid-back, And that same smirk I remembered from his speech.

I hit "*follow.*"

He accepted right away.

I ran back to the girl the next day like, "*Girl, you were right! He followed me back!*"

What I didn't realize until a whole month later— after a trip out of town and forgetting I even had Instagram notifications off-was that he had actually messaged me the next day after I followed him.

A full 30 days later, I opened my DMs and there it was:

"*Hey. Sorry it took me a minute to accept.*

Wasn't sure if it was really you."

I blinked. Stared at the message like it was glowing.

I messaged back instantly:

"*Oh my God-I'm just now seeing this 30 days later. Forgive me! I'm barely on here too.*"

He replied quick: "*No worries. How about we exchange numbers? I'm not big on social media anyway.*"

I didn't hesitate. Sent my number. And just like that...

The door opened.

He called the next morning.

I was halfway through my makeup routine, standing in my robe with a hot curling wand in one hand and my phone lighting up on the sink.

His name wasn't even saved yet—it was just a number. But I knew.

I tapped the screen with a little smirk already tugging at my lips.

"*Hello?*"

His voice hit me like warm honey. *"Good morning. I'm not interrupting anything, am I?"*

I looked at myself in the mirror, one brow half-done, hair pinned up, lips bare. Interrupting?

Please. He could interrupt me mid-prayer and I might still answer with "hey you."

"Of course not," I said smoothly. "I can multitask.

I'm just getting ready for work."

"Ah," he said, that low voice stretching into something that sounded like a smile. *"I wasn't sure if you'd respond at all. I figured after that thirty-day delay, you were blowing me off."*

I laughed softly, curling another piece of hair as I leaned into the counter. *"I wasn't. I promise. I really don't be on Instagram like that."*

"Well," he said, "I'm glad you finally saw the message... *because I meant what I said.*"

I paused, heart ticking up just slightly. "Which part?"

"*That you're aesthetically pleasing,*" he said without a drop of hesitation. "*I mean... you're just beautiful.*"

I had to look away from the mirror because I couldn't stop smiling.

"*Well,*" I said, trying to hold on to my composure, "*you're pretty easy on the eyes yourself.*"

There was a little pause on the line -one of those warm, charged silences where you both feel something unspoken pass between you. A mutual awareness.

"*Glad we agree,*" he said finally, voice dipped low.

"You caught my attention a long time ago, you just didn't know it."

"Is that so?"

"It is."

His confidence wasn't loud or performative. It was smooth. Grounded. Like he didn't have to convince me—he just needed me to know.

And damn if it didn't work.

We talked for over an hour that morning.

What started as a casual check-in turned into a full-blown vibe. No awkward pauses, no surface-level small talk-just him and me, trading pieces of our stories like we were meant to catch up on a connection the universe had delayed on purpose.

Somewhere in the middle of me curling my hair and laughing into the phone, he asked me, "*Is there anything specific you want to know about me?*"

I smiled into the receiver, curling the last strand. "*Just tell me whatever you want me to know. Like how old you are, what you like to do for fun...*

just more about you."

His response came smooth, steady-no hesitation.

"*I'll answer anything,* and ***I'll never lie to you,***" he said. "That's one thing about me. I love to travel.

Sports have literally been my life since I was five.

I'm a homebody unless I'm out of town. I like

going out to eat, catchin-a movie, or a show. never in my life had alcohol or smoked anything

—not once. I have two daughters, three grandkids. I coach lil league football. And.."

He paused for a second, just long enough to shift the energy.

"I was married for over 20 years before I lost my wife.

She was my everything."

My chest tightened a little. Not out of jealousy, but because I could hear the love and grief still laced in that memory. He wasn't just talking facts

—he was letting me see him. And in this day and age? That's rare.

"*Feel free to share too,*" he said gently. "Only what you're comfortable with, though. And just so you know, I'm super private. I don't like people in my business, and I really don't care for social media. *Hope that wasn't too much.*"

"*Not too much at all,*" I said softly. "That was honest. And I like that."

So I gave him my truth too.

"Well... I'm a mom of three. They're my heart. My everything. I love to travel too, and I'm a homebody for real. It's just work, church, home...

and shopping of course," I added with a little laugh

He chuckled. "Oh yeah?"

"Yeah, I love to shop," I said playfully. "And I'm trying to get into sports, but honestly? It's like Greek to me."

He laughed again-deep, rich, and genuine.

"And no alcohol for me either.

I mean, I tried a little weed when I was younger and thought I was gonna die."

"Oh, you dramatic," he teased.

"I mean seriously," I laughed. "It was tragic.

Never tried it again. Scarred for life."

I hesitated for half a second, then let the rest out.

"*And I'm going through a divorce.* After sixteen years."

The line got quiet for just a second. Then he said,

"I can tell you love and adore your kids. And wow, we gotta get you into sports for real,

because you're-missin' out.

I smiled.

"And that story about you almost dying from weed? That took me out, love the dramatics" he said, still laughing.

"But seriously... *I'm sorry to hear about your divorce.* I can't even imagine."

Then his tone shifted again-lower, more serious.

"**May I be honest?**"

"*Please*," I said. *"Be honest."*

"*You are so damn sexy to me,*" he said. "*I'm sorry, but I had to say it.*"

"*Don't be sorry,*" I said softly.

"*I told you-I speak my mind.*"

"*And I told you-I love honesty.*"

"*Okay then.*" He paused.

"So what do you wanna know that I haven't answered?"

"*I love honesty,*" I said again, just to let it sit between us.

After that, we slid into the conversation of how we ended up at the same job, what we do, how long we've both been there. It was effortless. No pressure. Just flow.

But then... I asked the question.

"Are you seeing anyone?"

He didn't pause. Didn't dance around it. Just said, *"Yes."*

Then added, *"I told you I'd never lie to you."*

And I believed him.

Surprisingly... I didn't flinch. Shit, He wasn't married, and he wasn't mine. He was single in my eyes— and the honesty? That was sexy all by itself. He gave me the power to decide if I still wanted to engage. And something about that kind of truth made me trust him more.

I remembered something I told my friend during my little search to track him down. I said, "***Even if it's nothing but sex, I'll take it. I just wanna lay with him.***" And I meant that. Even if this never turned into love.

Even if all we ever shared was chemistry, honesty, and passion behind closed doors...

I could live with that.

Because I just had to feel his touch

And for the first time in a long time, I had a crush and I felt wanted. Chosen. Seen.

After that call, something just... clicked.

We started texting every morning without missing a beat.

Good morning, beautiful.

Good morning, handsome.

Have a great day.

You too.

Simple. Consistent. Comforting.

And somehow, it became the best part of my day.

One morning, mid-convo, he said something that stopped me in my tracks.

We were talking about the way life unfolds

"You know," he texted, *"I believe everything in life happens for a reason. Like some people are born on days that others pass. Or they share dates with something meaningful. I don't think it's random."*

I stared at the message, goosebumps crawling up my arms before I even replied.

Today's date... He told me was his mother's birthday. A fact he shared so casually. not even knowing how it would land with me, because for me... today was the anniversary of the day my father passed away.

I texted him back: "*Wow... this is the day my dad passed.*"

There was a pause in the conversation—a weight that neither of us needed to explain.

The synchronicity wrapped itself around me like a whisper. Quiet. Personal. And undeniable.

It was just a moment. Just a shared date.

But for me... it was an inkling.

A soft nudge in the back of my mind that this connection was meant to be.

Maybe not forever.

Maybe not the way fairy tales promised.

But meaningful?

Absolutely.

Chapter Three: The Way He Touched Me

For weeks, their morning and night texts became routine.

Good morning, beautiful.

Good morning, handsome.

Sleep well?

I did. Have an amazing day.

You too.

And at night:

Goodnight, gorgeous.

Goodnight, king.

It was easy. Comfortable. And yet, something between them was shifting.

One afternoon, as they texted back and forth, the vibe got too good-so good it made Naomi check herself.

"It's just too soon," she texted.

"Too soon for what?"

"Too soon for these emotions I'm feeling toward you."

Legend didn't hesitate. *"Listen. Naomi...* ***we're human. You know that, right?"***

Her heart jumped at the way he said her name.

She couldn't help but think about how he would feel holding her. But she played it safe. Kept her cool.

That was... until she saw him again.

((The Hug That Changed Everything))

A few days later, they were at work
in the break room, sitting on
opposite ends of the room.

They weren't supposed to be
looking at each other.

But they were.

Every time she glanced up, his
eyes were already on her. And
when he looked away, she found
herself searching for him again.

It was like a magnet.

And as the meeting end

Naomi made sure she was in the
walkway so that.... he'd have no
choice but to pass by her.

As he did, time slowed.

The entire room faded,
background noise disappearing
into nothing.

He leaned in, his voice low, warm. *"Hello, how are you?"*

And then-his arms wrapped around her, pulling her into a full embrace.

Her breath caught.

His lips brushed close—too close-to her ear. His scent surrounded her, deep and masculine. And his warmth? Lord, his warmth spread straight through her body like wildfire.

She was tingling everywhere.

And when she slipped into the bathroom moments later, she realized just how much he affected her.

She was wet.

No one had done that to her in years.

So as soon as they were off work, she texted

"It was so nice to see you today and feel your warm embrace."

His reply was instant.

"I was just about to text you the same thing.

Very nice seeing you. You looked beautiful today... and you smelled good."

She giggled, fingers flying over her screen.

"Thank you. I found myself rubbing your back intently... then I had to tell myself, 'Girl, you better stop before people notice.'"

"I definitely felt you rubbing my back."

The air between them was thick with tension, unspoken but undeniable.

And later that night, when they fell back into their usual texting routine, the conversation took a turn neither of them expected.

((Desire Unleashed))

It started with little things.

A question here. A tease there.

But soon, the words between them were no longer innocent.

They talked about pleasure-what they liked, what they wanted.

Naomi admitted it had been three years since she'd had sex.

Legend confessed his current woman couldn't handle him in the bedroom.

"She says I'm too much," he told her. "I'm well-endowed."

Naomi rolled her eyes at the screen, smirking.

Yeah, okay. All men say that.

"I would never lie to you," he told her.

*"**It's big**"*

And ***it's thick.***"

Her stomach flipped.

Dangerous territory.

Then he asked, *"So what do you do to please yourself then?"*

She hesitated before replying. I'm trying to figure out how to respond to that.

Take your time he said.

*"**Well, let's just say —I have a little friend named Rose.**"*

His laugh came through the phone.

"Oh yeah, I've heard about that vibrator. Is she a good little friend?"

"A friend to the end," she joked.

And then...

"You really surprised me when you hugged me earlier," she admitted. *"I love the fact that you took initiative."*

His reply came instantly.

"Yeah, I'm a grown-ass man. I'm too old to play games, and not much makes me nervous."

She bit her lip, heart pounding.

"What were you thinking during the hug?"

"I won't lie. I wanted to feel you, not just through a hug. I thought about what it would be like to kiss you... what your body would feel like if I caressed it with my mouth."

A shiver ran down her spine.

"Is that too much?" he asked.

"*No*," she typed back. "*Not at all.*"

"*I have to be mindful,*" he continued. "*We're at work, and I don't like people in my business.*

But damn... my mind wandered."

"Mine too."

"How does your body react?"

She exhaled, heat rushing through her.

"*Like a wave of warmth flowing through me. And yours?*"

His response made her thighs press together.

"*Thoughts of you lead to stimulation... a vivid daydream. But at night?*"

She swallowed hard. "*Trust me, I know what you mean.*"

 The tension was unbearable now.

So she asked, "*What's your love language?*"

"*Physical touch.* Yours?"

Her breath hitched. "*Oh my God. That's mine too.*"

She knew then-this was dangerous.

And yet, she couldn't stop.

The Late Night Call

Their texts got hotter.

Bolder.

Until finally, he admitted, he was jerkin off and said *"I want to cum."*

She didn't hesitate. "***Cum, baby. Cum, handsome. I hope it's a lot.***"

"*It's always a lot.*"

She could barely breathe.

"**Selfishly, I want you to hear me,**" he said.

Her body tightened.

"**Then let me hear you.**"

And just like that, the text thread ended - replaced by a call.

She answered on the first ring.

The moment she answered, she could hear it— slow, wet strokes and the soft, rhythmic sound of skin gliding over skin. He was already moaning, deep and breathy.

"*Mmm... it feels so good,*" he groaned.

"**Does it feel good, baby?**" she whispered.

"*Yes...*" he breathed out.

"Oh baby, keep stroking it until you cum. I want to hear you cum."

"*You wanna hear me cum, Naomi? You wanna hear me cum?*"

he asked, his voice ragged with lust.

"**Yes**," she said, breath catching in her throat.

"*Then tell me what you're gonna do to it.*"

She smirked, her voice dropping into a sultry tease. "**I'm gonna spit on it and then I'm gonna sit on it. Imma ride that dick and squeeze it inside this tight creamy pussy.**

I'm gonna make it feel real good."

"*Damn, baby... you gonna lick my nipples too?*"

"Mmhmm," she moaned.

"**I'm gonna lick your nipples...**

then I'm gonna kiss all the way
down your stomach...

and kiss all around your balls until
you explode."

"*Damn... I'm about to explode now.
You wanna see it?*"

"**Yeah**."

"*FaceTime me.*"

She hit FaceTime. And when the
screen opened

-Lord have mercy.

There he was: that sexy, caramel,
fit man laid out on the bed.
Tattoos lined the side of his arm
and traced down his stomach. His
chest rose and fell with heavy
breaths as he stroked the biggest,
thickest dick she had ever seen.

It was stiff. Hard. Pulsing.

And he was stroking it slow and

deep, precum glistening at the tip.

She stared, mouth open, heart pounding, pussy throbbing. Something inside her snapped.

She started licking her lips. softly moaning.

"*Stroke it, baby... stroke it.* I wanna see it spit all over you."

He grunted, still stroking.

I'm gone fuck the shit out of you when I get you.

She couldn't hold it anymore.

She flipped her phone, pointed the camera at her thick, juicy ass, and started twerking-slow and deliberate, ass bouncing perfectly in the frame.

"**Damn, Nae... damn!** *So fucking sexy. You gonna make me cum...*"

She started smacking her ass,

grinding in circles, whispering,
"Cum, baby... cum for me. Cum for me..."

And just like that, he lost it.

"I'm cumming... oh, fuck, I'm cumming..."

His body jerked, dick throbbing in his hand as a thick stream of cum exploded-landing across his stomach, his chest, even up to his neck. It was a full release.

Loud, messy, uncontrollable.

She gasped, laughing through a moan. *"Oh my fucking God. That's a big ass dick."*

He groaned, still catching his breath.

"You made a whole mess, baby," she teased.

"Now you gotta clean that shit up."

They both burst into laughter, still high off the moment.

But even as they laughed, Naomi was already plotting.

I gotta have him, she thought to herself.

Even if it doesn't turn into anything serious...

Even if it's just a fuck...

I'm going to have this sexy-ass man.

Legend had been gone on a work trip and she counted down the days until he returned, the ache between her thighs a constant reminder of what they hadn't yet done. When his text finally came-"Good morning, beautiful. How have you been? I missed you." —she felt that familiar pulse of anticipation.

"I've been good, thinking about you," she replied. "I missed you too. What are you doing today?"

"Nothing, just at my second job."

"I'm coming to see you," she typed without hesitation.

"Really?" he replied with a laughing emoji.

"*Yeah, I need a hug. Is that okay?*"

"*Of course. I'll send you my location*"

As soon as he did, she was in motion - showering, shaving, making sure every inch of her skin was soft and smooth. She knew she wouldn't be able to take him right there in the office, but she had to feel him, even if just for a second.

When she arrived, the reality hit her. An open office.

Coworkers at their desks.

No privacy.

Damn, she thought. There goes my plan.

Still, the way he looked at her when she walked in, the long intimate hug, those hungry eyes devouring her like he already had her bent over his desk, made it worth the trip. They talked-about their trips, their weeks, their plans-but under the surface, tension crackled like static electricity.

Then, his hand slid onto her thigh. A slow, possessive stroke.

Her breath caught.

Then he pulled her onto his lap, his thick length pressing hard against her from beneath.

"Oh my God," she whispered, her pulse spiking.

His fingers traced lazy circles along her inner thigh. She bit her lip, trying to suppress a moan.

It had been such a long time for Naomi, that even that felt like ecstasy.

He reached down, unzipped his pants, and she started grabbing his dick.

It was so thick her fingers could barely wrap around it.

Truth is... she wanted to get on her knees and suck it right there in his office, she wanted to feel it in her mouth-but she couldn't.

He slid his hand in her pants and started rubbing her clit.

"Damn," he said, *"You are so wet."*

"Oh my God. I want you so bad."

His voice deep, rough.

She said, *oh yeah? Prove it*

"Who's at your house right now?"

Her stomach clenched.

"Nobody. My kids are at school."

He stood immediately, gripping her wrist, his decision made. **"*Let's go.*"**

No hesitation. No second-guessing. He told his staff, *"I'm stepping out for lunch,"* and they were out the door.

At Her House ...

((The Scene of Destruction))

The second the door closed behind them; they were on each other like a sex scene in a movie. Clothes ripped, breathless kisses, the heat between them unbearable.

He lifted her effortlessly, dropping her onto the couch, his body pressing her down, claiming space between her legs. His lips trailed from her collarbone down to her breasts, tongue flicking over her nipples until she trembled.

His voice was husky, laced with desire. *"You ready for me?"*

Her body answered before she could, a needy moan escaping her lips. *"Yes."*

He kissed his way lower, lower, until his mouth was exactly where she needed him to be. His tongue circled around her swollen clit, like he was spelling his name with it. slow and deliberate, teasing before devouring. She arched, legs shaking, the pleasure unraveling her.

"**Fuck**," she gasped, fingers gripping the couch.

"Oh my God, I can't"

"You can," he murmured against her, licking deeper, hungrier.

Her body convulsed, every lick sent her body to heaven and back, the climax crashing over her like a tidal wave, fast and hard, her moans raw and unrestrained.

But he wasn't done.

He stood up

Pulled out that big ass dick

Big Zaddy

He flipped her over, pressing her into the couch cushions, his thick tip teasing her entrance before thrusting in, stretching her, filling her. She cried out, nails digging into the upholstery.

He groaned, gripping her hips. **"Damn, this pussy is so fucking good."**

Every stroke touched her soul,

hitting deeper, harder, she could feel it in her stomach, sending ripples of pleasure through her & pulled her back against him, one hand gripping her breast, the other sliding down to play with her swollen clit as he thrust deeper. Juices was spilling everywhere.

She was gone.

Mind blank. Body wrecked. He was much bigger than what she saw on face time.

And he wasn't no minute man either. He lasted, keeping her on the edge, making her beg, until finally, with a deep growl, he buried himself inside her one last time, his body shuddering as he released.

They collapsed against each other, their skin slick, breaths ragged.

She lay there, spent, the scent of sex thick in the air

This man...

This man knew his way around a woman's body.

Knew how to use every inch of himself.

She'd never had anything like this before.

And she knew...

One thing for certain.

She wanted more

She had to have him again.

Even if it was just a fuck.

Chapter Four: Dick on Delivery

After that—it was kind of normal.

They went back to texting.

Back to their weekly phone sex.

FaceTime, stroking, moaning—at least twice a week.

It did not matter where she was at. She would always make time when he called to have phone sex with him, she talk real freaky, saying all types of nasty kinky shit to him, he loved for her to tell him what she wanted to do to him or what she wanted him to do to her and she would keep going until he released.

They had a routine now.

A rhythm.

And then one day... he called her from his office

Hello love ,what you wearing, you got a dress on?

I sure do, she replied

Then she quickly sent him a picture of her bent over the chair with her dress lifted up a little so he could see her thong.

Next thing you know,

He showed up at her floor.

She had an office to herself.

He stormed in like a man on a mission, one hand gripping her hair, the other sliding around her waist. His tongue licking the curve of her neck, making her knees weak. He bent her over the desk without a word, tugging her red lace panties down her thighs and putting them in his mouth like a trophy. Then, without hesitation,he sank his thick shaft into her dripping heat and began to fuck the shit outta her. Yes, right there.

In the damn conference room.

It was so damn good.

He had her gasping, bent over, choking her, spanking her, had her biting her lip—until one of her workers came knocking on her office door.

She had to pull her dress down fast, fix her hair real quick.

She shouted,

"I'm in a meeting—I'll come get you when I'm finished!"

As soon as the footsteps faded, he bent her right back over, no hesitation her body was to his command. One leg hiked up on the table, he drove himself in slow like he was trying to savor the moment, then deeper, then harder. Each stroke going deeper... and deeper...until she swore she could feel it in her damn ribs.

"I had to get this dick in you today," he said.

"I can't stay away from you too long."

"Big daddy had to come fuck the shit out of his lil hoe".

With your freak ass

It was a little disrespectful. A little wild.

But coming from him?

It turned her on.

"Now say it. Say 'you a hoe for me.'"

"You know I'm a hoe for you zaddy," she moaned.

She was moaning so loud he had to cover her mouth, it was crazy.

They released together and he left.

Chapter Five: When the Silence Felt Loud

After that, things shifted.

He'd ghosted her before-but this time was different.

Naomi could feel it in her gut. It wasn't just him being busy, or one of his usual disappearances for a couple days before popping back up with a sexy message or a late-night FaceTime.

No-this was silence.

Extended. Heavy. Confusing.

After the last time he bent her over the desk at work and gave her a pounding that left her thighs trembling through a full staff meeting, she thought they were on a new level. Thought maybe the intensity meant something to him, too.

And for a while, it did.

They kept texting. Kept connecting. Phone sex twice a week. FaceTimes where he stroked that thick, perfect dick just for her. Moments where he whispered things like:

"You got me sprung."

"I ain't never met someone who matched me like this."

"You're in my head."

And she was. Deeply.

But then... he disappeared again.

No good morning. No "what you wearing?" texts.

No FaceTime requests. Just... air.

Naomi tried not to overreact at first. Told herself she was trippin. That he'd reach out. That he always did.

But this time, her messages

weren't even delivering.

Blocked?

Her stomach turned at the thought.

Had she done too much? Was he done with her?

No answers came, and that silence grew louder by the day. So she did what she always promised herself she wouldn't: she pulled away. Quietly. Painfully.

She stopped checking for him.

Stopped looking at old messages, trying to protect her heart.

Started numbing herself to his absence.

But what she didn't know was on the other side of town, Legend was going through some shit.

He hadn't stopped thinking about her. Not for one day.

Not for one damn hour.

If anything, she was in his mind more now than ever.

The sex? Yeah, it was fire. The best he ever had.

No competition. But it wasn't just about the sex anymore-and that was the problem.

He liked her. Too much.

And that was dangerous.

His girl at home had started picking up on the shift. Asking questions. Watching his patterns.

Checking his tone. Hell, one night she reached for his phone while he was in the shower, and he had to make up some lie about work calling. After that, he blocked Naomi's number-not to be cruel, but for survival.

He thought it would be temporary

just a few days

Just until things settled.

But days turned to weeks.

And still... he thought about Naomi.
Every day.

*Her laugh. Her voice. That way she
moaned his name like a prayer and
a curse at the same time.*

*He thought about her lips. Her
softness. Her freak. The way she
rubbed his nipples like she'd
known him forever. The way she
made him feel like a man-desired,
needed, chosen.*

And most of all... he thought about
how she made him feel like he was
hers. Which scared the hell out of
him.

**Because it wasn't just lust
anymore. He was catching real
feelings. Feelings he hadn't
allowed himself to feel since he**

lost the love of his life. And that was a line he never meant to cross.

Naomi saw him. Not the coach. Not the emotionally guarded.

Not the man playing house with a woman who couldn't even keep up with him in bed.

Naomi saw all of him —and still wanted him.

So yeah, he stayed away. Not just because his girl was suspicious. But because he was scared that if he let Naomi in any deeper, he wouldn't be able to go back.

But the silence between them was killing him.

And when he finally got the courage to unblock her number and reach out... her energy had changed.

She didn't respond right away.

Her replies were shorter.

The playfulness was gone.

He felt it instantly.

That distance. That wall. That subtle shift that said: you don't get to have all of me after giving me crumbs.

And when they finally ended up in each other's arms again, all that fire, all that tension-it exploded.

She was moaning under him, nails digging into his back, and that's when it spilled out of him in a breathless growl:

"Don't ever fucking take yourself away from me again".

She froze for a second.

Eyes locked on his.

Breath caught between words.

"Then stop ghosting me like I'm disposable," she whispered.

That hit him like a punch to the chest.

He kissed her. Deep. Hard. Desperate.

"I didn't ghost you. I didn't...

I had to block you... **She got suspicious**. I ain't want to risk it. But Naomi... I never stopped thinking about you. Not once. I didn't know how to deal with this. With you." She stared at him, vulnerability flickering behind her fire.

"Then just say that. Don't leave me hanging like I imagined it all."

His hand cupped her face, thumb brushing her cheek.

"You didn't imagine shit. You are in my head now, Nae. I just didn't know what to do with it."

Chapter Six: Come Correct or Don't Come at all

Naomi had changed.

She still thought about him. Still felt her body react when his name popped up. Still remembered the way his mouth tasted, the way he whispered *"You're my bitch"* with the kind of hunger that made her lose all sense of time.

But she wasn't making herself easy anymore.

So when Legend started texting again-more frequently this time, trying to slide back in like nothing ever happened-she didn't match his energy right away.

"Good morning, beautiful."

She read the message and left it there for a beat.

Then an hour later:

"Morning."

One word. Cool. Simple.

He felt the shift.

He knew her energy used be soft
and warm,

full of emoji kisses and have a
great day king

Now? It was guarded.

And it drove him crazy.

He couldn't lie-he missed her.
Missed her voice, her mouth, her
body, her attitude. The way she
gave him sass and sweetness all
wrapped in one sexy little package.

He hadn't touched Naomi in weeks,
and nothing he tried filled that void.

Not even his woman at home
could fill it.

Truth be told, he'd been avoiding

sex with her altogether. it was boring, it wasn't the same and It never would be again.

Because his body-and maybe his heart-was somewhere else now.

With Naomi.

He craved Naomi...

So he called. Texted. Tried to joke his way back in.

"Hey you, I was just thinking about you."

"You must be tired, running through my mind like that lol."

"I need to see that smile again."

She'd reply... but it wasn't the same.

And when he finally called and she actually answered, his heart thudded in his chest harder than he expected.

"Hey stranger," she said, dry but polite.

"Don't do me like that," he said with a soft laugh. *"You know I've been... going through some things."*

"Yeah. *You've gone through your texts and my number too,* apparently," she said.

"You went missing, Legend."

He sighed. **"Naomi... I told you. It wasn't because I didn't want to talk to you."**

"No? Then why?"

Silence.

Then he admitted it.

"Because this started, as something casual.

But now you're in my head. And I didn't know how to handle that. I didn't expect to feel... this."

Her breath caught for a second.

"This?" she echoed.

"You," he said. "I felt myself falling for you. And I'm already with someone who's been through hell with me. I didn't want to lose everything.

But I couldn't lose you either. So, I got scared. I shut down."

The line was quiet for a long moment.

Naomi's throat was tight. Her heart? Tired.

"You don't get to come in and shake up my world, make me feel seen and desired again, and then disappear like it never happened," she said. **"That shit hurt, Legend.** *I'm not just some side chick with a vibrator and free time.*

I'm a whole woman, with feelings".

"I know that" he said softly.

"Damn, I know that."

"Then act like it," she whispered.

That night, she laid in bed, her phone screen dimly lighting the room. Her heart was still racing from the conversation. Her chest tight, her thighs tingling. She hated how badly she still wanted him.

The phone buzzed again.

Legend: **"I meant what I said. I want you Nae."**

She stared at the message.

Didn't type back.

Didn't smile.

She just lay there, reading it over and over.

And in her mind, the words started repeating like a spell she couldn't break:

"This was just supposed to be a pleasure contract..."

"This was just supposed to be a pleasure contract..."

No strings, no feelings...

"But... **DAMN, I think I love him."**

TO BE CONTINUED ...

The Sequel

Consequences Of Chemistry

You thought it ended with Naomi
facing reality? Not even close.

She thought she could handle it.
That she could keep her feelings in
check, keep her body in control,
keep her heart out of it.

But love has a way of slipping in
through the cracks—

And Legend?

He's already under her skin.

Now the game is changing.

Boundaries are blurring.

Jealousy is brewing.

And secrets?

They're harder to keep when bodies are addicted and hearts are involved.

When feelings grow where they were never supposed to...

Somebody always pays the price.

Will Naomi continue to play the role of the one who waits in the shadows?

Or will she demand to be seen, heard, and chosen?

And Legend...

Will he finally stop fighting the truth, or will his fear of losing everything push her away for good?

Let's Be Real: Reflections from the Pleasure Contract

This ain't your average book club section. These are grown folks' questions—for the ones who've lived, messed up, fallen hard, or tried to keep it casual and got caught up anyway.

Take a deep breath. Grab a pen. Let's unpack it.

Have you ever convinced yourself it was "just sex"? Be honest—was it really? Or did you secretly hope for more?

_____
_____
_____
_____
_____
_____
_____
_____
_____
_____
_____
_____

What did you tell yourself to justify being the side? Was it about freedom? Power? Control? Or did it just feel good to be wanted again?

_____
_____
_____
_____
_____
_____
_____
_____
_____
_____
_____
_____
_____
_____
_____
_____
_____
_____
_____
_____

Did you ever catch feelings and not know what to do with them? What did that shift look like—did it scare you? Did you run? Did you stay?

_____
_____
_____
_____
_____
_____
_____
_____
_____
_____
_____
_____
_____
_____
_____
_____
_____
_____

Have you ever stayed quiet about
your needs to avoid "doing too
much"? Did you minimize your
worth to protect his ego—or your
heart?

_____
_____
_____
_____
_____
_____
_____
_____
_____
_____
_____
_____
_____
_____
_____
_____
_____
_____

What cost did your silence come
with? Did you lose sleep? Yourself?
Your peace?

_____
_____
_____
_____
_____
_____
_____
_____
_____
_____
_____
_____
_____
_____
_____
_____
_____
_____
_____

If you could write your own
"pleasure contract," what would be
in the fine print now? What would
you never allow again? What would
you require without apology?

_____
_____
_____
_____
_____
_____
_____
_____
_____
_____
_____
_____
_____
_____
_____
_____
_____

And finally... was it worth it? That fire, that thrill, that escape—what did it teach you? What did it leave you with?

_____
_____
_____
_____
_____
_____
_____
_____
_____
_____
_____
_____
_____
_____
_____
_____
_____
_____
_____
_____

" Every pleasure
has its price...

This one just came
with feelings."

Reflections

[redacted]

Join the Conversation

Got a pleasure contract of your
own?
Still tangled in an entanglement?
Or maybe... you're ready to draft up
a new one.

I want to hear from you.

Share your story, ask your
questions, or just drop a note.
Let's talk intimacy, boundaries,
heartbreak, lust and everything in
between.

Reach out directly at:

🌐

www.ThePleasureContract.com

✉️

vannahreign@thepleasurecontract.com

Let's keep the conversation and
the connection going.
Everybody needs somebody to talk
to sis.
We listen and we don't judge lol
We connect. Hit me up.

JPAY AND CORRLINKS FRIENDLY.